Purple Class
and the Flying Spider

D0532911

For Ben with his flowers and his horizons,
and with thanks to George and Stan.

Sean Taylor

Purple Class and the
Flying Spider
and other stories

Illustrated
by Helen Bate

FRANCES LINCOLN
CHILDREN'S BOOKS

Purple Class and the Flying Spider copyright © Frances Lincoln Limited 2006
Text copyright © Sean Taylor 2006
Illustrations copyright © Helen Bate 2006
Cover illustration copyright © Polly Dunbar 2006

First published in Great Britain in 2006 and in the USA in 2007
by Frances Lincoln Children's Books, 4 Torriano Mews,
Torriano Avenue, London NW5 2RZ

www.franceslincoln.com

Distributed in the USA by Publishers Group West

British Library Cataloguing in Publication Data
available on request

ISBN 10: 1-84507-627-3
ISBN 13: 978-1-84507-627-6

Printed and bound in the United Kingdom by Bookmarque Ltd

1 3 5 7 9 8 6 4 2

Contents

Purple Class
and the Flying Spider

Ivette raced out of the classroom. Zina was so close behind her that they almost fell over each other.

"It's following us!" hissed Zina.

Ivette reached back and slammed the classroom door with a loud bang.

Along the corridor, Mr Wellington was leading the rest of Purple Class back from lunch.

"What was *that*?" asked Jamal.

Mr Wellington turned the corner with a serious look on his face. Ivette and Zina were standing there.

"Was that you slamming the classroom door?" he asked.

Zina nodded.

"No way am I going in that classroom again," said Ivette.

"Why?" asked Mr Wellington.

"There's a flying spider in there," Ivette told him.

"A *what*?" asked Leon. He looked through the glass in the door. So did Jamal.

"It had quivery legs and beady eyes!" muttered Ivette.

"Everyone back in line!" said Mr Wellington. "There's no such thing as a flying spider."

"There is such a thing as a flying spider," announced Shea. "I saw it on TV."

"That must have been a horror film," Mr Wellington told him.

Shea shook his head.

"It was a nature programme about the jungle, and it showed how a flying spider bites your throat if you don't dive and roll."

"The flying spider tried to bite Zina," nodded Ivette.

"Quiet!" Mr Wellington told them. "I don't know what Ivette and Zina saw – probably just a large fly or a bumble bee. But I'm going into the classroom. And, unless I fall over clutching my throat, I suggest you follow me."

He pushed the door.

"If you see it, dive and roll," advised Shea.

Mr Wellington stepped inside. The classroom was very still.

"Nothing," said Jamal, from the doorway.

"Whatever it was has gone," nodded the teacher. "It's probably already halfway back to the jungle. Now let's get on with our afternoon."

In ones and twos, the children came in through the door. Shea and Jodie covered their throats with their hands.

"Right!" called out Mr Wellington. "Ivette, what did I send you and Zina in here to do?"

"You said we had to tidy up the classroom because it looks as if a grizzly bear has been sleeping in it," said Ivette.

"Yes," said Mr Wellington. "It's Parents'

Evening tonight, and look at the mess in here. You're supposed to be our Tidying-Up Monitor, Ivette!"

"We were doing more than just tidying up," Ivette told him. "We were doing an express makeover."

"An *express makeover*?" repeated Mr Wellington.

"If you harmonize the furniture and sort out the clutter crisis, it changes the whole energy flow of the room," said Zina.

"It improves everyone's talent and wisdom," added Ivette.

"Well, I'm glad you want to improve everyone's talent and wisdom," said Mr Wellington, looking around. "But the place still looks a right mess to me. There's a used tissue, a satsuma skin and a plastic octopus from the Creepy Creatures Activity Set on the floor.

Someone's PE kit is in the box of laminated digit cards. And look at your tray, Ivette. It's like an erupting volcano over there!"

"We only got as far as harmonizing the furniture in the Reading Corner. Then the flying spider shocked us," said Ivette.

"Well, that means there's still a lot to do before your mums and dads arrive. So we're going to have *15 minutes* at the end for a big tidy-up."

There were nods from the children.

"Good," sighed Mr Wellington. "Now, that's plenty of chit-chat. Let's get back to our science topic."

"Endangered Species," said Yasmin.

Mr Wellington nodded.

"This afternoon you're going to do some artwork using the Endangered Species Panel."

He pulled a tall stand-up panel towards the carpet. There were facts and photographs on it. He told the class he wanted everyone to choose one of the animals on the panel. He asked them to find out five key facts about the animal they chose, and write them in their science books. Then he said that they could do either a painting or a clay model of their animal.

Soon the children were clustered around the Endangered Species Panel. Shea chose a snow leopard. Jodie chose a Colombian yellow-eared parrot. Ivette chose a tropical butterfly fish.

"Can I do a chipmunk?" asked Leon.

Mr Wellington looked at the panel.

"There isn't a chipmunk on here," he said. "It isn't an endangered species, Leon."

"I know," said Leon. "But I like chipmunks. And no one else is going to do one. So I feel sorry for it."

Mr Wellington sighed.

"I want you to choose an endangered species, Leon," he said.

"All right," said Leon, looking at the panel. "I'll do a Chinese crocodile newt."

★★★

Ivette was one of the first to finish writing. She took her science book to show Mr Wellington. He was picking things up off the floor. He had the used tissue, the satsuma skin and the plastic octopus in one hand. He threw the tissue and the satsuma skin in the bin. Then he took Ivette's book.

"That's fine," he said, looking around for somewhere to put the plastic octopus. "Now, get yourself some paper and you can start a painting."

Ivette reached down to open the paper drawer. As she did so, the flying spider fluttered out.

"AAARGH!" she shrieked, swerving out of its way.

There were gasps as the flying spider spiralled up towards the middle of the classroom, then screams as it started coming down again. Somebody bumped into Mr Wellington's desk, sending his pen pot flying, and his jar of paperclips on to the floor. Shea dived and rolled. The PE kit that was in the box of laminated digit cards fell on the floor. Then the laminated digit cards tumbled on to the floor as well.

"It's only a daddy-long-legs!" shouted Mr Wellington, holding up a hand for silence.

Some of the children looked at him, but others were too busy trying to work out where the flying spider had disappeared to.

The noise only died down when Mr Wellington barked out, "WILL YOU PLEASE BE QUIET? I can't hear myself think if everyone's chattering away like a hundred waterbirds!"

He put the plastic octopus on the top of the computer table.

"A daddy-long-legs looks like a flying spider, but it's not. It's a completely harmless insect," he said.

"I wish it was an endangered species, whatever it is," murmured Ivette.

"Quiet!" said Mr Wellington. "You've got to stay calm in these situations otherwise there could be an accident."

"There *was* an accident," said Jamal. "Look at your desk."

Mr Wellington turned round and saw the mess.

"RIGHT!" he said. "I'VE HAD ENOUGH! You've got half an hour left for your artwork. If you can't do it sensibly we'll forget about art, and just do tidying up."

Ivette walked back to her table with the others. They sat down with barely a scrape of their chairs.

"No talking. No interruptions," said Mr Wellington. "And if a whole family of daddy-long-legs appears and starts doing Irish dancing up and down the radiator you're going to ignore them."

Nobody dared to laugh.

★★★

The children got on with their painting and clay models. Nobody disturbed Mr Wellington as he picked up the laminated digit cards and put everything back in place on his desk. And there was almost complete silence as he came across to take a look at their work. He said he liked Jamal's clay mountain gorilla.

"You can almost hear it going *WOOH! WOOH! WOOH!* can't you?" said Jamal.

"Yes, Jamal," Mr Wellington replied.

On the next table, Yasmin showed Mr Wellington the clay rhinoceros she was making, and Ivette held up her painting of a tropical butterfly fish.

"That's a very colourful fish, Ivette," Mr Wellington told her, "but I can't tell which end is the head and which end is the tail."

"Don't you like modern art?" asked Ivette, with a playful grin.

Mr Wellington smiled for the first time in a while. Then he told the class, "Looking around, I can see some good work! But we've got 15 minutes left now, and you've got a promise to keep!"

"Tidying up," said Leon.

Mr Wellington gave the children different jobs. Ivette reorganized her tray so that it would shut. Jamal put the pots of paint on the tall table by the sink. Zina swept the floor with a dustpan and brush.

After a time, Mr Wellington said, "This is looking better. Now, I've got a letter to photocopy for your parents. Can I trust you to keep going until I get back?"

"It's going to look even better when you get back," said Ivette.

"Good," said the teacher, and he went out of the door.

Ivette straightened up a few desks. Then she spotted a pencil under one of the computer table's legs. As she bent down to pull it out, the table gave a wobble and the plastic octopus fell on to her head. Ivette stepped backwards, trying to feel what it was in her hair. But Zina was crouched just behind her with the dustpan and brush. Ivette crashed into her and toppled sideways. She stretched out a hand to grab the table. But Ivette's hand hit Yasmin's art board, which was sticking over the edge of the table. Yasmin's clay rhinoceros was flipped into the air.

"What's in my hair?" yelled Ivette.

Zina was laughing. Yasmin was laughing. Everyone was laughing except Ivette.

"It's only the octopus from the Creepy Creatures Activity Set," said Yasmin.

"It felt like a flying spider doing Irish dancing," frowned Ivette.

Yasmin bent down to pick her art board off the floor.

"Where's my model?" she asked.

"There!" called Jamal. He was pointing towards the ceiling.

"Oh no!" said Yasmin.

Ivette put a hand over her mouth. The clay rhinoceros was stuck to one of the top windows.

"Sorry, Yasmin," she said.

"Mr Wellington is going to have to do Parents' Evening with a clay rhinoceros above him," said Leon.

"It'll probably drop on someone's head," said Yasmin.

"My mum's a beautician," said Ivette. "She'll go mental if she gets a clay rhinoceros in her hair."

"Someone's got to get it down or Mr Wellington's going to get white-hot under the collar," said Zina.

Everyone agreed, but they couldn't decide how to get the clay rhinoceros down. Jamal said he could probably make it fall down by giving the wall a karate kick. But all he did was hurt his toe. Jodie said they could suck the rhinoceros down if they got a vacuum cleaner. But Shea told her it would block the vacuum cleaner and make it explode.

Then Ivette announced, "I'm just going to climb up! If I get on the window ledge I can reach it."

"That's high," said Shea.

But Ivette had already made up her mind.

★★★

The class helped Ivette take the scissors rack, the ruler jar and the paint pots off the tall table by the sink. They put everything out of the way on Mr Wellington's desk. Then they put the tall table under the window with a chair on top of it. Ivette climbed on to the table, then on to the chair. That way she managed to get one knee on the window ledge and pull herself up.

"Careful!" exclaimed Zina.

But Ivette was already standing upright. She stretched out a hand and prodded the clay rhinoceros. There was a cheer as it came unstuck. Some children reached out to catch it, but all they did was knock Mr Wellington's jar of paperclips on to the floor again. The clay rhinoceros landed in Mr Wellington's mug.

"Take it out of there!" whispered Ivette, rolling her eyes.

"Get down!" called up Shea.

Ivette reached out a foot. But it hit the back of the chair and knocked it sideways. Next thing, the chair was tumbling off the end of the table and falling, with a crash, on Mr Wellington's desk. Scissors and plastic rulers scattered across the desk and on to the floor. All but one of the paint pots tipped over. Ivette looked down with her eyes wide. Orange, green, red and yellow paint was running in all directions.

Somebody said, "Clear it up!"

Somebody else said, "Mr Wellington will be back!"

But he was already back. In he came with the photocopies in one hand.

"I could hear you right down the corridor, Purple Class..." he said. Then he stopped.

His paperclips were on the floor again. There were scissors and rulers in a puddle of paint on his desk. And Ivette was standing on a window ledge.

"What on earth's happening?" he asked, dropping his photocopies on the chair behind his desk. Everyone looked at Ivette.

"We were trying to get the classroom tidy, Mr Wellington," she said. "But a rhinoceros flew up and stuck to the window..."

"Ivette!" interrupted Mr Wellington. "Explain later! I've just seen your mum and dad. They're coming as soon as the bell rings, and I don't want them to find you halfway up the wall talking about flying rhinoceroses!"

"I'm trying to get down," said Ivette.

Jamal picked up the chair and put it back on the table. Ivette cautiously reached out her foot.

"Wait! That's dangerous! I'll get on the table and lift you down," said Mr Wellington, and he clambered up on to the table.

"Now?" asked Ivette.

"Hold on!" said Mr Wellington.

He glanced down to make sure that his feet were steady but, when he looked up, Ivette was already stepping off the window ledge. He reached out his hands and caught her. But he was off balance. The two of them started to topple over.

Once they had started, there was no stopping them. There were gasps from the children.

Zina called out, "You're falling off the table, Mr Wellington!" But it didn't help.

Ivette closed her eyes. And, in slow motion, she and Mr Wellington dropped with a BOOM on to one of the Reading Corner bean-bags. It burst like a balloon, sending a cascade of polystyrene pellets up into the air. The children put their hands over their heads. White pellets scattered across the floor. There was a chaos of voices on the carpet. Mr Wellington got to his feet looking rather like a snowman.

He brushed at the bean-bag pellets on his face and checked that Ivette was all right. She was. Then the bell went.

"Oh no!" said Mr Wellington. "Leon! Try to delay Ivette's mum and dad."

"How shall I delay them?" asked Leon.

"Talk to them," said Mr Wellington.

"What shall I talk about?" asked Leon.

Mr Wellington rubbed his nose.

"Anything," he said. "Chipmunks."

Leon went out of the door.

Ivette looked round the classroom.

"It looks worse than if a grizzly bear has been sleeping in it now," she said.

"It looks as though the grizzly bear woke up and invited all his friends round for a tag wrestling contest," said Shea.

"We'll never clean my desk in time," said Mr Wellington.

"You could do Parents' Evening in the corridor," suggested Yasmin.

Mr Wellington shook his head.

"We could clear up the things on the floor, then hide your desk behind the Endangered Species Panel," suggested Ivette.

Mr Wellington nodded.

"Good idea," he said. "But I need everyone's help, *fast*."

Some of the class picked paperclips, scissors and rulers off the floor. Others gathered handfuls of polystyrene pellets. Ivette and Shea lifted the Endangered Species Panel and put it in front of the teacher's desk. With the desk hidden and the floor cleared, the room looked surprisingly normal.

Mr Wellington caught sight of Leon with Ivette's mum and dad in the corridor.

"Thank you for helping," he said to the class. "Tomorrow you can explain to me how such a gigantic accident happened. For now, off you go."

All the children, except for Ivette, filed out. Her mum and dad were coming in. Mr Wellington smiled.

"Did Leon look after you?" he asked.

"Sort of," said Ivette's mum. "He told us we had to answer a riddle, for security reasons."

"Oh," said Mr Wellington, trying to keep smiling.

"Who fries the potatoes in a monastery?" said Ivette's dad.

Ivette and Mr Wellington shrugged, as if to say they didn't know the answer.

"The chip monk," said Ivette's dad.

★★★

Mr Wellington tried to make it a completely normal Parents' Evening meeting. He said he admired Ivette's determination, although she could sometimes be better at doing exactly what she was told. Ivette's mum and dad nodded. Everything went fine. Then Mr Wellington said he had a letter for them. He got up and reached behind the Endangered Species Panel. And that was when the daddy-long-legs surprised him. It fluttered into his face, making him step back into the Endangered Species Panel.

"Sorry," he said, as the small creature bounced off a blind and disappeared out of an open window. "Just a daddy-long-legs."

But Ivette was looking at something else.

"Behind you, Mr Wellington!" she said.

The teacher looked round, but it was too late. The Endangered Species Panel was swaying over. It dropped, with a light thud, on the carpet and Ivette's mum and dad stared at the teacher's desk. On it were overturned paint pots, scissors, rulers, mixed up streaks of coloured paint, white polystyrene pellets and a clay rhinoceros in a mug.

Mr Wellington looked as though he had just swallowed a screwdriver.

"That's the art project we're doing," announced Ivette.

"That's an art project?" said her dad.

Mr Wellington sat down. Several polystyrene pellets fell out of his hair.

"Don't you like modern art?" he asked.

The Vanishing Violins

Leon was late. He came down the corridor with his PE bag on his back and a huge dustbin liner in his arms. The dustbin liner was so full that he could barely see where he was going.

"Who's *that*?" asked Zina, as the bulging, black shape came through the door.

"Looks like some sort of swamp monster!" said Shea.

"It's Leon!" said Ivette.

Leon put the dustbin liner down by the coat hooks, and everyone could see who it was.

"Sorry I'm late," said Leon.

He looked at the front of the class, expecting to see Mr Wellington. But it was Miss Zanetos, Orange Class's teacher, standing there.

"Hurry up and sit down, Leon," Miss Zanetos told him. "Mr Wellington has had a problem with his car, so everyone's doing quiet reading until he arrives."

Leon sat down.

"Mr Wellington's car's *old*," said Jodie.

"That thing should be in a museum," added Shea.

"All right, Purple Class, quiet!" said Miss Zanetos. "I have to see how my class is getting on, but I'll be back."

Jamal put up his hand and asked, "Can I put on my *Sweet Beats To Move Your Feets* CD? It's good for quiet reading concentration."

Miss Zanetos shook her head as she walked towards the door.

"Quiet reading means quiet, Jamal," she said.

Leon opened his PE bag to find his reading book. One blue trainer fell on the floor. Then he slowly pulled something long and white out of the bag. It was one of his mother's bras.

"Look!" he said, holding it up. There was a roar of laughter. Jamal wrinkled his nose and turned his face away.

"That's big!" said Ivette.

"Not as big as my nan's bra!" said Zina. "You could use hers as a tent!"

The door swung open. It was Mr Wellington, looking hot.

"What's going on?" he asked.

Leon blinked.

"Miss Zanetos told us to do quiet reading," he said.

"Well you're not doing quiet reading, Leon," said Mr Wellington. "You're holding a bra in the air. Where did you get that?"

"It's my mum's," said Leon. "It was in my PE kit by mistake. I don't want it."

"Give it to me then," said Mr Wellington, impatiently, and there was another burst of laughter as he took the bra and stuffed it into his trouser pocket.

"That's enough!" he said. "I've got a headache and the day hasn't even started."

Mr Wellington walked across to his desk and put down his bag.

"I'm sorry I'm late," he said. "I had a problem with my car."

"Did you crash it?" asked Jodie.

"No," said Mr Wellington. "It broke down."

"That car's *old*," said Jodie.

Ivette nodded.

"It embarrasses us, seeing our teacher get into that car," she said.

"Even the windscreen wipers go slowly," pointed out Jamal.

"Right!" said Mr Wellington. "That's enough about my car. We've got much more interesting things to do. First of all, spelling words. Then, after break, Mrs Powell from the *Strings for Schools* project will be paying us a visit."

"To teach us violins," said Yasmin.

Mr Wellington nodded.

"Are we each going to have a violin?" asked Jodie.

"Yes," said Mr Wellington.

"As a free gift?" asked Leon.

"Just to borrow," Mr Wellington told him, staring towards the coat hooks. "Now what's that enormous bag at the back of the class?"

Leon looked round.

"It's plastic bottles I brought for the recycling campaign," he said, proudly.

"The recycling campaign was *last* week, Leon," Mr Wellington said. "The lorry has probably taken the recycling container away by now."

Yasmin shook her head.

"It's still in the playground," she said.

"Well," said Mr Wellington. "You'd better get your bottles into it before they *do* take it away."

Leon nodded and put up his hand.

"How much do you think all the bottles I've brought are worth?" he asked.

"I don't know," said Mr Wellington.

"Would it be closer to one pound or 100 pounds?" asked Leon.

Several children around the classroom started giving their opinions and Mr Wellington had to put up his hand for quiet.

"Listen, Leon," he said. "Your bottles won't be worth a gooseberry unless they're in that recycling container pretty quick. So take them across now. And someone's left some old boxes in the

Downstairs Hall. Put those in as well while you're at it."

"All right," said Leon.

He picked up the dustbin liner, accidentally knocked the Creepy Creatures Activity Set on the floor and went out of the door.

For the next half-hour, the children in Purple Class worked with their spelling partners. Jamal said the words gave him a headache. But for the first time ever he got all of them right, and Mr Wellington was pleased. The class was finishing for break when Leon came back.

"You've been gone for ages, Leon," said Mr Wellington.

"Sorry," shrugged Leon. "It was all those boxes. I had to go backwards and forwards and forwards and backwards like a tennis ball."

"Like a rather slow tennis ball," said Mr Wellington.

Then the bell went.

★★★

After the children came back from break there was a firm knock on the classroom door. It was Mrs Powell. In she came, wearing a brown dress with a sparkly pattern on the skirt.

"Hello, Mr Wellington," she said, putting her handbag on his desk.

"Nice to see you again," nodded Mr Wellington. Then he turned to the class and said, "Mrs Powell is kindly going to repeat the violin lessons that she gave to Purple Class last year."

The violin teacher looked at the children and smiled.

"And Mr Wellington is kindly going to make sure that there is *no* repeat of what went wrong last year," she said.

Mr Wellington rubbed his ear.

"Yes," he nodded. "Last year there was an unfortunate accident with a violin."

"Last year somebody *sat* on a violin!" said Mrs Powell.

"It was my brother's friend, Callum," said Shea. "He's an under-12s rugby player."

"What did the violin look like after Callum sat on it?" asked Jodie.

"It looked like a violin that had been sat on by an under-12s rugby player!" answered Mrs Powell.

"But," added Mr Wellington, firmly, "there will be no repeat of that this year because you are all going to be extra specially careful with the violins."

The children nodded.

"Good," said Mrs Powell. "Now, has anyone here ever played a violin before?"

Nobody nodded.

"Does anyone come from a musical family?"

The children stared at her.

"Come on," said Mr Wellington. "Who's got a musical instrument at home?"

Jamal put up his hand.

"I've got a guitar," he said, "but it hasn't got strings, so it's not much good, except for hitting my friend Bradley with."

"I see," said Mrs Powell. "Well, thanks to the *Strings for Schools* project, you are now all going to get a real taste of music."

She explained that the class would be having six violin lessons with her. She told them that they would be working towards a violin performance at the end of term. Then she looked round the children and asked if there was anything more they wanted to know.

Leon's hand went up.

"When they recycle plastic bottles, what do they actually do to them?" he asked.

"Mrs Powell meant, are there any questions about music," Mr Wellington told the class.

Jamal put up his hand.

"Have you heard a CD called *Sweet Beats to Move Your Feets*?" he asked.

"No," said Mrs Powell. "Now I think it's time we went through to the hall."

★★★

The children brought their chairs, and soon they were sitting in a circle in the Downstairs Hall.

"Right," said Mrs Powell. "The violins?"

Mr Wellington nodded. Mrs Powell glanced around.

"Where are they?" she asked.

"Oh," said Mr Wellington. "You said you were having them delivered."

"I had them delivered," said Mrs Powell, "to the Downstairs Hall."

"This is the Downstairs Hall," pointed out Ivette.

"Well, they must be here somewhere," said Mr Wellington, standing up.

He peered under the benches and looked up on the stage. But there were no violins.

"Don't worry," said Mr Wellington, trying to

smile. "Things like this happen in a busy school."

"It's never happened in any other busy school," she said.

"It may be a case of *spontaneously vanishing*," suggested Shea. "It happened to my pyjamas. I couldn't find them. My mum couldn't find them. They just spontaneously vanished."

"Thank you, Shea," said Mr Wellington. "But I think we'll find there's a more straightforward explanation for the missing violins."

"Someone might have locked them in the PE cupboard," suggested Jodie.

"Yes!" said Mr Wellington, brightly. He felt in his trouser pocket and pulled out his keys. Unfortunately, the bra came out as well. Mrs Powell blinked as it dangled from the teacher's key-ring. The children tried not to laugh.

"So sorry!" said Mr Wellington. "It's not mine. It's Leon's mother's…"

He was going to say something else, but decided not to. He put the bra back in his pocket and unlocked the door, saying, "This is where the violins will be."

The door opened. Inside there were football-training cones. There were basketballs, rounders bats and plastic cricket stumps. But no violins.

"Can we play cricket instead of violins?" asked Jamal.

"This is quite unacceptable!" said Mrs Powell. "I can understand someone losing a pencil or a glove. But how on earth could you lose 30 violins?"

"I don't know what's happened," Mr Wellington told her.

"Well, you should know what has happened," said Mrs Powell. "Have they been stolen? Have they been sat on by a rugby team? Have they been beamed up by an alien spacecraft?"

Mrs Powell reached into her handbag and took out her mobile phone.

"Are you going to call the police, Mrs Pow-wow?" asked Zina.

"No," said the violin teacher. "I'm going to call our delivery man."

She put the phone to her ear and walked across the hall.

As she did, Leon put up his hand.

"Can I say something, Mr Wellington?" he asked quietly.

"Is it important?"

"Perhaps," said Leon.

"Go on then."

"Were the violins in black boxes?" asked Leon.

"I expect so," Mr Wellington replied.

Leon nodded.

"Then I probably made a big mistake."

"What did you do, Leon?" asked Mr Wellington.

"I'm sorry," said Leon. "It makes me want to go to the South Pole and live with penguins. I gave the violins to the recycling campaign."

Mr Wellington closed his eyes.

"I thought the violins were the old boxes you told me to take to the recycling container," explained Leon.

Mr Wellington opened his eyes to see where Mrs Powell was. She was still talking loudly into her phone.

"Mrs Pow-wow will go mad if she finds out," said Yasmin.

"She's not called Mrs Pow-wow," said Mr Wellington. "She's called Mrs *Powell*. A pow-wow is a Native American dance festival."

But that was all he had time to say, because Mrs Powell finished her phone call and came walking towards them.

"Mr Wellington," she said. "Our van driver has just confirmed that the violins were *definitely* delivered here this morning."

"Yes they were," smiled Mr Wellington. "In fact, everything is now solved. A message has arrived saying that the violins were accidentally moved elsewhere. So I'm going to take Leon, Zina and Shea, and we shall fetch them."

"Good," said Mrs Powell.

"Meanwhile," said Mr Wellington. "I suggest that Ivette organizes a quick game of ZIP, ZAP, BOINK."

The children were happy about that. Mrs Powell didn't look quite so keen. But, moments later Mr Wellington, Leon, Zina and Shea were heading out of the hall and Ivette was explaining the rules of ZIP, ZAP, BOINK to Mrs Powell.

★★★

As soon as Mr Wellington and the children were through the door, Leon started hopping from foot to foot.

"If we get the violins Mrs Powell won't ever know what I did!" he said.

Mr Wellington nodded and whispered, "Try to act normally until we get round the corner and out of sight of the hall."

They tried to act normally. But the moment they went round the corner, there was a terrible silence. The recycling container had gone.

"Oh no," said Leon.

"It was there at break," said Zina.

"I think I can feel a stress-related illness coming on," said Mr Wellington.

"The lorry must have only just left," said Shea.

"There's going to be a solution if we think quickly," said Mr Wellington.

"I've thought quickly," said Leon. "My mum

can maybe afford to buy some new violins. I think you can get them cheap on the Shopping Channel."

"No," said Zina. "I've seen this in a film! You've got to chase after the lorry in your car, Mr Wellington!"

Mr Wellington did think about it. But then Shea reminded him that his car had broken down.

"The caretaker, Mr Furlong, might be the best one to help," suggested Leon.

"Yes, Mr Furlong was in charge of the recycling container," Mr Wellington said. "He'll have a phone number for the lorry driver! Come on! We'll go back the way we came and see if he's in his room."

As they turned the corner, Leon called out, "There it is!"

The lorry, with the recycling container on it, had pulled up by the side entrance to the school. The driver was standing with Mr Furlong, signing a piece of paper.

"We've got to stop him!" said Shea.

"Yes, but we'll have to pass the hall without Mrs Powell seeing us," hissed Mr Wellington.

"Duck down!" said Zina.

They did. Leon, Shea and Zina ducked, even though none of them were tall enough to be seen

through the hall windows anyway. Mr Wellington
bent over so much that his hands almost touched
the ground. Slowly they passed along the length
of the hall.

As they passed the last window, Zina
whispered, "Done it!"

"Easy as kicking pebbles on the beach!" said
Mr Wellington, looking towards lorry.

But that was when a pair of legs appeared. It
was a pair of legs in a brown skirt with a sparkly
pattern on it. Shea and Zina jumped. Leon put his
hand up to his mouth. Mr Wellington looked as
though he had come face to face with the
Abominable Snowman.

"Do you need some help?" asked Mrs Powell.

"We were just crossing the playground," said
Mr Wellington, standing upright.

"Why are you crossing the playground when you're meant to be fetching the violins?" Mrs Powell asked.

Mr Wellington's tongue seemed to have stopped working. So Leon said, "We've just got to very quickly check what's in the recycling container."

"Check what's in the recycling container?" echoed Mrs Powell.

Mr Wellington nodded. "Yes," he said.

"We've got to count how many plastic bottles fit into it," said Leon. "It's for a project."

Zina and Shea nodded seriously.

"It's part of a Science Topic called *What fits in a box?*," added Mr Wellington.

He looked through the window of the hall and could see the rest of the class happily playing ZIP, ZAP, BOINK.

"What about the violins?" asked Mrs Powell.

"Someone is going to deliver them in just a little while," said Leon.

"Yes," said Mr Wellington. "So wouldn't you like to go back and have another game of ZIP, ZAP, BOINK? It looks quite fun."

"No thank you," said Mrs Powell. "I can't think of anything I would like to do less that play another game of ZIP, ZAP, BOINK."

Leon looked across the playground. The driver was climbing into the lorry.

"I think we've got to get over there," he said.

"Excuse us for a moment," said Mr Wellington, and he, Leon, Zina and Shea ran towards the lorry waving their arms.

Within moments the driver was helping Shea and Zina to count plastic bottles. Meanwhile Mr Furlong and Leon went round the back of the lorry and lifted the green lid of the cardboard section of the container. Leon's eyes lit up when he saw the violins exactly where he'd left them.

"Right, you daft old doughnut," said Mr Furlong. "Leave this to me."

"We never did modern subjects like this in my day," smiled the lorry driver, as Mrs Powell arrived.

Mr Wellington explained to Mrs Powell in some detail how the *What fits in a box?* topic enabled the children to measure dimensions, calculate volume and estimate capacity.

"*Wotsits in a box* is one of our favourite subjects," said Zina, trying to help.

Mr Furlong fetched his trolley. Round the back of the lorry, Leon helped him load the violins on to it. Mr Furlong covered them with a plastic sheet. Then he set off across the playground, whistling as if he didn't have a care in the world.

★★★

There were smiles all round when Mrs Powell and the others arrived back from the playground and saw the violins neatly spread out across the stage in the Downstairs Hall. She was very keen to start the lesson.

Mr Wellington just had time to say quietly to Leon, "That must be the least sensible thing you have ever done in your life."

Leon shook his head.

"Dropping my mum's mobile down the toilet was less sensible," he said. Then he asked, "Is your headache better now, Mr Wellington?"

The teacher stopped and thought for a moment.

"It is actually, Leon," he replied. Then, as Mrs Powell handed out the violins, he added, "But I'm expecting it to start up again at any moment."

Goodbye Joyce

There was a new member of Purple Class. The children called him Bad Boy. He was a white and tan guinea-pig. First thing on Monday morning Shea, Yasmin and Bad Boy were the only ones in the classroom. The two children were supposed to be giving the guinea-pig his food and water.

"He likes cool music, you know," said Shea, taking a CD out of Jamal's tray. "When Jamal plays this, Bad Boy nods his head."

Yasmin turned down her mouth.

"He nods his head all the time," she said. "He's nodding it now. Look."

She unhooked the guinea-pig's water bottle and took it over to the sink.

"But he does *funky* nodding if the music's cool," said Shea, striding over to the CD player.

"*Sweet Beats to Move Your Feets* isn't even cool," said Yasmin.

"This is *Smoove Moves To Make You Groove*," said Shea.

The CD started up with a mix of beats and booms. Bad Boy carried on nodding his head.

"See!" grinned Shea. "When the rhythm gets Bad Boy rocking, check out the way he does *funky* head nodding."

He turned the volume right up and started jabbing a finger towards the hutch in time to the rhythm. The classroom door opened and Mr Wellington walked in.

Shea was enjoying himself so much that he didn't notice. He almost jumped out of his skin when Mr Wellington shouted, "Shea! Turn that off!"

"Sorry," Shea said, trying to find the OFF switch. "It's not my CD. It's Jamal's."

"Well, you're the one playing it," Mr Wellington told him. "You're the one dancing around as though you've got ants in your pants. And you're the one supposed to be doing something completely different."

"We're feeding Bad Boy," said Yasmin.

"I know," said Mr Wellington, "and I want you to get a move on with it. The school has had some very bad news. I've got a meeting in the staff-room, and you two need to get back to the playground."

"I've changed the water already," Yasmin told him.

"And I'm giving Bad Boy his food," said Shea.

"Well give him his food double-quick, Shea," said Mr Wellington, following Yasmin out of the door.

Bad Boy sniffed at Shea's hand as he opened the clip on the hutch door. Shea took out the little food bowl. He tipped seed mix into it. Then he put it back. It was all done double-quick. In fact it was all done *so* double-quick that Shea forgot to close the clip on the hutch door.

There was a good game of football going on in the playground. The teachers didn't come to take Shea and the others in until five minutes after the bell. Back in the classroom Mr Wellington took the register. Then he said, "Listen. I'm sorry to say we received some very sad news over the weekend. It's about Joyce."

"Our dinner lady, Joyce?" asked Jodie.

"Yes," nodded Mr Wellington. "She was taken seriously ill on Friday after school. Her husband took her to hospital and she was very well looked after. But she died on Friday night."

The children looked upset. Zina stared straight ahead without blinking. Jamal looked at his fingers.

"Poor Joyce," said Ivette.

"I know you'll all be sad," said Mr Wellington. "I'm sad. All the teachers are."

"Joyce liked Bad Boy," said Jodie. "She always came and gave him carrots."

"She did like Bad Boy," said the teacher. "She liked all of us. We've lost a friend. So, we're not going to start our morning with Mental Maths. Instead, we're going to give everyone a chance to say something about what's happened. Is that a good idea?"

The children nodded.

"Mental Maths is hard anyway," said Shea.

"Talking about someone dying is pretty hard," said Mr Wellington. "But it's one thing we can do to make ourselves feel better."

He asked the children to push back the desks and sit in a circle. Then he took a piece of paper out of his bag. It was a photograph of Joyce at Christmas Dinner. The children looked at the picture as Mr Wellington stuck it to the wall.

"She's wearing flashing-on-and-off reindeer horns," pointed out Ivette.

"She's laughing," added Jodie.

Mr Wellington nodded and sat down.

Leon said, "She's dead."

There was quiet for a moment. Then Ivette asked, "What are we meant to say?"

"Well," Mr Wellington told her, "it's up to you. You might say something nice about Joyce, or you might like to say something about how you feel."

Jamal put up his hand.

"If Joyce died," he said, "I wonder if we're going to get our dinners today."

"The school might have to get a Chinese takeaway," said Leon quietly.

Mr Wellington shook his head.

"Don't worry," he told them. "You'll get your dinners."

"I want to say goodbye to Joyce," said Zina.

"Well," said Mr Wellington, "later this morning there's going to be a chance to say goodbye. Joyce's funeral procession is going to pass the school and, if any of you want to, you can go out in the playground and see it."

All the children said they wanted to go out in the playground to see the funeral procession. Then they said things they remembered about Joyce. Someone said she was kind. Someone said she wore big glasses. Someone said she made the best spaghetti.

When it was Shea's turn, he said he used to see Joyce's husband dropping her off in the morning in his red car.

"If he saw you he always raised his hat and smiled," he added.

"He'll be lonely now," pointed out Ivette.

"He will," agreed Mr Wellington.

Then Yasmin said, "But at least Joyce won't be old any more."

Mr Wellington nodded.

"She had a fantastic life," he told the class. "She loved working in this school. She lived to 70. A guinea-pig like Bad Boy only lives for four or five years."

"That's not fair," said Shea, looking round at Bad Boy's hutch.

"Where *is* Bad Boy?" asked Jamal.

"Bad Boy's probably tucked into his bedding," said Mr Wellington, looking back at the circle of children.

"He's not," said Yasmin.

Mr Wellington frowned and got up.

"He's not in there," said Jamal.

Mr Wellington looked in the hutch.

"Perhaps Joyce took him with her," suggested Leon.

"She *didn't* take him with her," said Mr Wellington. "Look. The door of the hutch is undone. He must have got out! Who fed him this morning? Shea and Yasmin?"

Shea put up his hand.

"It was me," he said, looking worried. "Maybe I left the door undone."

"Now Bad Boy is probably dead too," said Jodie.

"I'm sorry," said Shea. "I didn't mean to do it."

"Let's stay calm about this," said Mr Wellington. "I'm sure we can find Bad Boy. He doesn't move very quickly."

"He does if he wants to," said Jamal. "He could have got all the way to the bus-stop already."

Mr Wellington held up his hand.

"Look," he said, "there's only 20 minutes before Joyce's funeral procession goes past and I think we should use that time to find Bad Boy. I'm sure that's what Joyce would have wanted us to do."

★★★

They searched the classroom first. Leon had a pocket-sized laser torch that helped them look behind shelves and cupboards. But there was no sign of Bad Boy.

"He's not in here," said Ivette.

"We'd have heard him snuffling," added Zina.

"Yes," said Mr Wellington. "Let's look somewhere else."

A pair of girls was sent to check the girls' toilets. A pair of boys was sent to check the boys' toilets. Zina and Shea knocked on the door of Orange Class to see if there was any sign of Bad Boy in there. The rest of the children stayed with Mr Wellington. He said they were going to search the corridor and told the children to walk from one end to the other, checking everything in their path.

Everyone took it very seriously at first. But then Leon started arguing with Ivette about whether a laser torch could blind a guinea-pig. The girls in the girls' toilet ran out saying they'd seen a cockroach. Several children disappeared into the Downstairs Hall and had to be fetched back, and Jamal decided to show everyone how far he could skid if he took his shoes off.

"Right!" said Mr Wellington. "This is no good! There's no point in searching unless we search quietly. And we can't all just do our own thing. We've got to be methodical."

"What does that mean?" asked Jamal.

"*Methodical* means we're organized and don't clomp about like a herd of water-buffalo on a hot afternoon!"

Jamal nodded. Zina and Shea came back from Orange Class.

"All we found in there was a photograph of a guinea-pig on the wall," said Shea.

"And it wasn't Bad Boy," added Zina.

"All right," said Mr Wellington.

He sent Leon to fetch the two boys from the toilets.

"Maybe Bad Boy has got down into the sewers," suggested Yasmin.

"There are hundreds of thousands of escaped guinea-pigs down in the sewers," Zina told her.

"Shhh," said Ivette. "Mr Wellington says we're

only going to find Bad Boy if we're quiet and metaphorical."

Zina pretended to understand.

★★★

The children followed their teacher into the Downstairs Hall. Mr Wellington split the class into groups and gave each one a different part of the hall to search. Almost at once, Ivette's group pointed excitedly behind the piano and shouted that they'd found Bad Boy. They tried to drag the piano away from the wall. But its wheels were stiff and, as they pulled, it started to tip over.

"Stop!" shouted Mr Wellington rushing across.

They stopped and the piano rocked back with a hollow thud.

"Honestly," said the teacher. "I've come across laundry baskets with more sense than you lot. We'll take a look with Leon's torch."

Leon shone his laser torch into the darkness and there was a sigh from the class. It looked like Bad Boy, but it was actually the head of an old broom, stuck behind the piano.

One disappointment followed another. From the other side of the hall Jamal called out, "He's here under the PE mats. He's squashed."

"He can't be squashed," said Mr Wellington, walking back across the hall.

"He's squashed flat," said Jamal.

Everyone looked anxiously, as three children lifted up the PE mats and Jamal pulled out a flattened shape. Then the silence changed into a burst of laughter. It wasn't Bad Boy. It was a pair of pants that had been there so long that they'd gone hard.

At the same moment Ivette started complaining that Leon was trying to blind her with his laser torch, and Mr Wellington shouted, "RIGHT! EVERYONE STOP!"

He confiscated Leon's torch and put it in his pocket.

"Bad Boy can't be in here," said Shea.

"I don't think he is," agreed the teacher.

"We've lost him," said Zina. "And Joyce would have been upset."

"If she'd seen Jamal with those pants she would have laughed about it," said Jodie.

Everyone agreed. Mr Wellington was going to say something but, just then, his phone rang.

"Sorry," he said, reaching into his pocket. "It'll be Mrs Sammy ringing from the funeral procession."

He took out Leon's pocket-sized laser torch

and put it to his ear. The children burst out laughing. Mr Wellington tutted and got out his phone instead.

It was Mrs Sammy, the Head Teacher. Mr Wellington spoke to her for a moment or two, then he said, "Right. We've got to call off this search. The funeral procession will be reaching the school in five minutes."

The children nodded.

"Now," went on Mr Wellington, "if you are going to come outside, I need you to be very grown-up."

The children stared back at him.

"Do you all know what a funeral procession is?" the teacher asked.

Some children nodded. Some didn't look so sure.

"It's those long, slow cars, isn't it?" said Shea.

"Yes," said Mr Wellington.

"My sister hired one for her eighteenth birthday," said Zina. "It was a limo with eight doors and three televisions."

"Those are long white cars," said Mr Wellington. "In this procession there's going to be some long *black* cars and Joyce's coffin will be in one of them."

The children nodded again.

"Now you don't have to go," said Mr Wellington. "But hands up who'd like come to the playground and see the funeral procession?"

All the children put up their hands.

"Right," said Mr Wellington and he led them out to the playground.

***

Several other classes were already gathered outside. Mr Wellington told Purple Class to stay together near the railings while he had a word with the other teachers.

"I feel sad twice," said Leon, when Mr Wellington came back.

The teacher nodded. Then he called for everyone in the playground to be quiet. The children listened.

"I'd like to tell you that Joyce would have loved to see you out here to say goodbye to her," said the teacher. "The funeral procession will go past any minute and I want you to remember that you are representing our school, so let's do it well. It's normal and respectful to stay *quiet* and *still* at a funeral, so that is what I'm going to ask you to do. Does everyone understand?"

The children nodded.

"Are there any questions?"

Leon put up his hand.

"Is it true that when you die you become grass?" he asked.

"We can talk about that later, Leon," said Mr Wellington.

There were no other questions. So the children stood and waited.

Only a moment or two passed and there was a huge scream. Shea and the others twisted round and they couldn't believe their eyes. Bad Boy was sprinting between the children on the far side of the playground. The screaming was followed by laughing and then more screaming. Some children backed away as Bad Boy came towards them. Some set off chasing after him. Bad Boy himself wheeled round and disappeared underneath the litter bin.

It took a very loud shout from Mr Wellington to quieten the children down.

"Stop!" he roared. "Ignore the guinea-pig! The funeral procession is coming right now! We can't have you jumping around like a lot of kangaroos! I want absolute silence!"

Some of the children stared up the road. Some of them stared at the litter bin. Everyone stood quietly. Mr Wellington looked at his watch. Then he looked at the children. Then he looked up the road. There was no sign of the procession.

"It's not coming," whispered Zina.

"They probably took a wrong turning and are going past the wrong school," suggested Leon.

"I asked for absolute silence," said Mr Wellington quietly.

No sooner had he spoken than Bad Boy shot out again. He came belting across the playground, straight towards the children in Purple Class. Mr Wellington looked at the guinea-pig. Then he looked at the children. Then he looked up the road. The first long, black car was coming round the corner.

"HERE THEY COME!" he bellowed. "FORGET ABOUT THE GUINEA-PIG. EVERYONE QUIET AND STILL!"

The children stared at the road and tried to stay quiet and still. But Shea didn't manage. Bad Boy was scampering right past him. He couldn't resist. He bent down. He reached out. He grabbed the guinea-pig safely in his hands. The children around him cheered and, at that moment, the funeral procession passed in front of the school.

Mr Wellington pressed his lips together and looked round. A long black car with a coffin inside and beautiful flowers on top went past. The children waved.

Jamal shouted out, "Goodbye Joyce!"

Leon shouted out, "Thank you for making all our dinners!"

Shea held up Bad Boy to say goodbye to Joyce too.

The car with the coffin rolled slowly on, and behind it were lots of other cars with people in. Joyce's husband was sitting in one of the cars, looking out of the window at the children gathered in the playground. When he saw them waving, he raised his hat and he smiled.

The Vegetable Patch

As the children followed Mr Wellington into the classroom one Thursday morning, there was lots of talk about Shea's haircut. He'd had it shaved round the sides, but it was spiky on the top like a punk.

"Did you pay someone to do that?" Jodie asked him.

Shea nodded.

"It's the latest style," he said.

"It looks like they cut it with a knife and fork," Jodie told him.

"Or a lawn-mower," suggested Ivette.

"Right!" interrupted Mr Wellington. "Interesting though it is, I don't want to stand around chatting about Shea's hair. We've got a rather special and exciting morning ahead, and I want to get on with it."

He took the register. Then he said, "Now. Have any of you noticed Mr Furlong digging over at the Wild Area?"

Lots of children nodded.

"I think it's an escape tunnel," announced Jamal.

Mr Wellington shook his head.

"It's a vegetable patch. We'll be going out there this morning to plant the vegetable seedlings you've been growing in the classroom."

Some of the children looked at the pots of vegetable seedlings in trays on the window-sill. They were labelled CARROTS, TOMATOES and BEETROOTS.

"That's not *rather special*," Jodie said.

"And it's not *exciting*," added Zina.

"It's gardening," pointed out Leon.

"Gardening's for nerds," said Ivette.

But Mr Wellington shook his head.

"All sorts of people do gardening," he told the class.

"Yeah," said Ivette, "But they're not normal people."

"It's not a properly educational thing for school," announced Jodie. "You don't *have* to grow vegetables. You can just get them out the fridge."

Mr Wellington let out a sigh.

"What would you rather do then, Jodie?" he asked.

"I'd rather stay in the classroom and play Zoombinis on the computer. It helps you learn maths, and that's more important than growing vegetables."

There were nods from some of her friends.

"Beetroots are just for grandmas anyway," said Ivette.

"Look!" snapped Mr Wellington. "You're actually going to learn a lot from growing vegetables. And I haven't even told you the *most* exciting part." He looked around the class. Then he said, "Yesterday I got an email from a TV company making a documentary about vegetable gardening in schools."

"And did you tell them about our beetroots?" asked Jamal.

Mr Wellington nodded.

"So they asked if they could film us today and I said they could."

There was a complete change on the faces of the children.

"A real TV crew?" asked Zina. "With cameras and everything?"

"Cameras and everything," said Mr Wellington.

"And is everyone going to be on TV?" asked Yasmin.

"Everyone except for Jodie, who wants to stay in the classroom and play Zoombinis," nodded Mr Wellington.

As the news sank in, there was a cheer from the class. Jodie put up her hand.

"Actually, I think I'd better come," she said. "Because I've already been on TV when we planted a time capsule, so I know what to do."

"Well, that's fine, Jodie," said Mr Wellington. "I'm sure you'll be a great help with your TV skills. Meanwhile you can be a great help with your carrying skills. We're going over to the Wild Area and you can carry the beetroots."

Mr Wellington got out two bags of trowels. He organized who was going to carry what. Then he told the children to line up by the door. Jodie picked up the tray of beetroot seedlings and pulled a face at it.

"You should have told us that the TV cameras were coming, Mr Wellington," she complained. "Then we could have got dressed properly."

"You look absolutely fine, Jodie," the teacher told her.

"I'd have gone for more of a rock-chick look if I'd known I was going to be on TV," she frowned.

Mr Wellington picked up a coiled, yellow hosepipe and said, "Right, that's everything. Any questions?"

Ivette put up her hand.

"Can we wear make-up?" she asked.

"No," Mr Wellington told her.

"What about cotton-candy flavoured lip gloss?" asked Yasmin. "I've got some in my tray."

"No," repeated Mr Wellington. "The TV crew want an ordinary class in an ordinary school, not a lot of people dressed up as if they're on their way to a wedding."

"It's not fair," said Jodie. "You have to wear make-up on TV. Even the Prime Minister does."

"I don't think the Prime Minister wears cotton-candy flavoured lip gloss," said Mr Wellington, leading the class into the corridor.

There was a lot of chatter as the children followed their teacher into the warm sunshine.

"It's good that we're going to be famous," said Jodie. "Up until now it's been Orange Class getting all the publicity. They had their photo in the paper, and they don't even know how to tie their shoes yet."

"You'll enjoy being on the TV," said Mr Wellington. "And you'll also enjoy some healthy eating when we pick our vegetables in a few months' time."

"I know about healthy eating already," said Ivette, who looked very much as if she was wearing cotton-candy flavoured lip gloss. "It means you don't eat sugary snacks and ready-prepared meals. You have a turkey sandwich with organic asparagus tips instead."

Mr Wellington nodded and opened the gate into the Wild Area.

★★★

Purple Class's vegetable patch was a rectangle of soil dug into the grass and divided into three sections.

"It's quite a nice place," said Jodie standing with one hand on her hip and looking around at the trees and the sky.

"Yes," nodded Mr Wellington. "Mr Furlong's done a good job hasn't he? It's a lovely sunny position, just right for growing vegetables. And it's *ours*. There are all sorts of things we can do. We might even have some fun and make a scarecrow."

"We don't need one," said Jodie. "Shea's haircut will scare away any crow in the world."

Mr Wellington organized the class into groups and handed out the trowels and the seedlings to be planted. Everyone in the first group got a pot with a tomato plant in it. Everyone in the second group got a pot with a carrot plant in it. Everyone in the third group got a pot with a beetroot plant in it. Each of the groups spread out round a different section of the vegetable patch. Ivette didn't want to be in the beetroot group, but Mr Wellington said she had to be. Jodie looked more cheerful. She was in the carrot group and she said carrots were the best.

Once they'd all found a space, Mr Wellington

knelt down and showed the children how to prepare the vegetable patch for planting.

"You clear away any stones," he told them, "and break up big lumps of earth with your trowels."

Jodie got the knack quickly. One or two of the others looked less sure. Jamal held his trowel with two fingers and prodded the vegetable patch with a worried look on his face.

"This muck's got germs in," he said.

"It's not *muck*, it's *soil*," said Mr Wellington. "And it won't do you any harm to get a bit of dirt under your fingernails."

"I'm not getting dirt under my nails," Ivette said. "Your nail care says a lot about you, you know."

Mr Wellington raised his eyebrows.

"Look," he said, "we've got visitors coming to make a TV programme about vegetable gardening. They'll be here any moment, and if they find us discussing nail care instead they'll probably go and film another school."

The children agreed and there was no more talk about nail care.

Mr Wellington showed everyone how to plant the seedlings. Some children asked questions about how to do it, but Jodie planted hers straight away.

Mr Wellington said she'd done it the right way, but the TV crew wanted to film the class doing the planting. So she had to carefully dig it up.

"Just carry on preparing the soil," nodded Mr Wellington. "I'm going to attach the hosepipe to the tap. It's a hot day and the seedlings are going to need some water."

He headed over to the playground with the yellow hosepipe. And that was when the TV crew arrived.

★★★

"It's them! They're here!" hissed Jamal.

The children stopped and stared as the TV people walked over to Mr Wellington and shook his hand. There were three of them. There was a smartly-dressed woman with a clipboard. There was a big man in an orange sweatshirt carrying a camera. And there was a smaller man wearing a brown suit.

"I'm going to carry on gardening," said Jodie. "We're live on TV."

But, as she spoke, her trowel hit something buried at the edge of the vegetable patch. She couldn't tell what it was, only that it was a long and rusty.

"What's this?" she asked.

Shea was kneeling next to her. He leaned over and looked. Then he pulled himself back.

"That's an unexploded bomb," he said. "They found one near our flats."

Jodie and several others stood up.

"What's a bomb doing in a vegetable patch?" asked Yasmin.

"It's from the war," said Shea. "It might be a German torpedo."

"Or a nuclear bomb," added Zina.

"But is it going to explode?" asked Jodie.

Shea nodded.

"If anyone touches that, it'll blow us to kingdom come," he said.

"We've got to tell Mr Wellington," said Leon.

"But if Mr Wellington knows about a bomb then there'll be an emergency and the school will have to be abandoned," said Jodie.

"He'll call the army in," pointed out Jamal.

"And we'll never be on TV," complained Jodie.

"They'll go to another school, or film Orange Class," said Shea.

That made the children think twice.

"It must have been here for centuries already without exploding," said Jamal.

"They're coming!" whispered Leon.

Jodie looked round. Mr Wellington was leading the TV crew through the gate into the Wild Area.

"*You* found it, Jodie, so you've got to decide what to do," said Zina.

"I'm not telling them," announced Jodie.

★★★

"Right," smiled Mr Wellington. "Let me introduce our visitors. This is the presenter, Sabina. This is

Terry the cameraman. And this is Gordon the programme director."

"Are you on Sky Sports News?" asked Leon.

Gordon shook his head.

"We're from the Teachers' Channel," he said.

Some of the children looked a little let down.

Ivette told Sabina that she, Zina and Yasmin could do a cool new dance if they were interested in filming it. Sabina thanked her but said they wanted to film the children planting vegetables and then interview them about why they liked gardening.

Terry stood his camera up on some adjustable legs and explained a bit about how it worked. Jodie asked Terry if you could play Zoombinis on it, and Jamal asked Terry if he could have his autograph.

But at that point, Gordon called out, "Listen up for a sec! We're going to do a shot of the beetroot group doing their planting, with Sabina saying her introduction just *here*."

Several children winced as Gordon pointed his finger right at where the bomb was.

"She can't stand there!" said Zina.

Gordon looked down.

"Why?" he asked.

There was a short silence. Then Jodie said, "Because of ants."

"We found an ants' nest there," nodded Shea. "And I think they're soldier ants. One of them bit Leon and he's been acting strangely ever since."

Gordon frowned at the ground. Then Sabina said, "I don't like ants, Gordon. I'll stand down this end."

"All right," agreed the director. "We'll make it a shot of the carrot group doing their planting, with Sabina standing at the other end."

There were grumpy looks from Ivette and the beetroot group as Terry picked up his camera and took it down to the other end of the vegetable patch. But there were completely horrified looks when the cameraman stopped right on top of the bomb. Worse still, he stamped his foot to see if the ground was firm enough to stand the camera on. Jodie swallowed. Shea stared with wide eyes. Leon pulled up the hood on his sweatshirt.

Terry noticed the children staring.

"I'm not worried about ants," he grinned.

"But don't stamp too much," said Jodie. "Soldier ants are an endangered species, you know."

Terry nodded and, moments later Gordon called out, "ACTION!"

Sabina looked at the camera and started saying her introduction. The children had to plant their seedlings. Gordon said he wanted everyone to look completely natural. But, in the first shot, Leon smiled at the camera. He did it again in the second shot and Mr Wellington had to tell him to grow up.

"I'm sorry," Leon said. "I just can't get the smile off my face."

The third shot went better. The only problem was that Ivette had planted her beetroot seedling upside down. But Gordon said that wouldn't matter, because it was only really the carrot group who would appear on the screen. The beetroot group got a bit sulky about that. But all the children were pleased to see Terry lift up his camera and move away from the bomb.

Afterwards, they did interviews and those went pretty smoothly. Ivette cheered up when she was chosen to do the first one.

Sabina asked what she thought of gardening and Ivette replied, "Some people say it's just for nerds. I don't agree with that. But I don't think I should be planting a beetroot seedling because beetroots are old-fashioned and taste like worms."

"What would you like to grow instead?" asked Sabina.

"Organic asparagus tips," Ivette replied.

There were a few small problems with Jamal's interview. He got so close to the camera that his nose touched the lens, and Terry had to wipe it clean.

Then Sabina asked him, "What's your favourite vegetable, Jamal?"

He said, "Mainly tomato ketchup."

And that made Terry laugh so much that the camera shook.

Jodie's interview was probably the best. First she said, "I think gardening is a very educational activity for our bodies and our minds."

It seemed a bit like she was trying to say the right thing, but Gordon gave her a big thumbs up. Then she said, "And I'm looking forward to seeing how my carrot plant grows up." You could tell she really meant it.

Gordon decided to finish with a shot of Mr Wellington watering the vegetable patch with the whole class watching. Mr Wellington seemed pleased that he was going to be on camera at last.

Terry filmed him turning on the tap and coming back across the playground with the yellow hosepipe but, unfortunately, the hosepipe did not stretch far enough. So the last shot was of him tugging at it and the children laughing. Mr Wellington wanted to film it again, but Gordon checked his mobile and said they had to rush off.

"Thank you," Gordon said. "You've been absolutely terrific, Purple Class."

Then they left.

★★★

Once the TV crew had gone there was a great chorus of opinions about what had happened and who had been best on TV. But Mr Wellington asked the class to turn their attention back to the vegetable patch.

"There's an unexploded bomb in there," said Jodie. "But I didn't tell you in case we didn't appear on TV."

"An unexploded bomb?" said Mr Wellington, furrowing his brow.

The children pointed to the spot where the bomb was.

"Who thought that was a bomb?" he asked.

Jodie thought for a moment. Then she said, "Everyone."

The teacher reached out a foot and prodded the bomb. Shea put his hands over his head.

"Don't touch it," said Ivette.

Mr Wellington turned down his mouth.

"That isn't a bomb. It's just a bit of old metal," he said, picking up one of the trowels. "Look, I can probably get it out with this."

He pushed the trowel into the ground and the piece of metal shifted. There was no explosion. Some of the children looked slightly disappointed. Mr Wellington gave the trowel another push. Then there was a crack, like a plate snapping. And it was followed by a great burst of sound. The air seemed to go thick and grey. The

children ran helter-skelter, in all directions. Shea dived and rolled. Mr Wellington stumbled backwards. Leon fell into the beetroots.

Jodie was halfway to the playground before she dared to look back. When she did, she realized that water was filling the air. It was spurting out of the ground in several different directions.

"It's all right!" said Mr Wellington, helping Leon to his feet. "It's a water pipe! I broke it!"

Yasmin was sent to fetch Mr Furlong.

"Sorry," Mr Wellington told the caretaker. "I seem to have broken a water pipe here."

"I can see that," said Mr Furlong, putting his hands on his hips and looking at the crack in the pipe. "I'm sorry too. I should have remembered that pipe when I dug the vegetable patch."

Mr Furlong turned off the water at the mains the gush of water slowed and stopped.

"Right," said Mr Wellington. "It's been quite a morning, hasn't it?"

The children nodded.

"But Mr Furlong has got everything under control, and the bell will be going for lunch, so we'll head indoors and get ourselves cleaned up."

He led the children back across the playground.

"Are you going to help Mr Furlong fix the pipe?" asked Jodie.

Mr Wellington shook his head.

"He's better at that sort of thing than me," he said. "I think I'll stay in the classroom and play Zoombinis on the computer."

Jodie smiled and turned back to look at the vegetable patch.

"The plants got watered in the end," she said.

"They did," agreed Mr Wellington. Then he added, "It'll be good seeing the TV programme, won't it?"

Jodie nodded.

"And it'll be good seeing the carrots."

"I think you quite liked gardening," Mr Wellington told her.

Jodie shrugged.

"I didn't know if I was going to rate it or hate it," she said. "But, in the end, I rated it."

Mr Wellington looked pleased.

"You can be a surprisingly good teacher at times," said Jamal.

They reached the school building, and Mr Wellington held open the door.

"What did you like about what we did?" he asked.

"Mainly the exploding pipe," said Jodie,

walking past. "You should put an exploding pipe in our lessons more regularly."

The rest of Purple Class followed her inside, and nodded their heads in agreement.

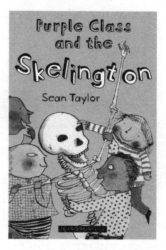

Read more about the adventures
of Purple Class in Purple Class
and the Skelington!

For over fifteen years Sean Taylor
has worked as a visiting author and storyteller
in schools, encouraging children to write
poems and stories. The Purple Class stories spring
directly from those visits and all the dramas
and funny things he sees going on in classrooms.
Sean is the author of many books for young readers
including *BOING!*, *When a Monster is Born*
and *Small Bad Wolf*. He wrote *Purple Class and
the Flying Spider* in the back bedroom of an
old house in Bristol. He and his wife moved there
after living for a long time in Brazil.
"Bristol and Brazil don't have much in common,"
says Sean. "But they do both begin
with Br and end with l…".

Purple Class and the Skelington

Sean Taylor
Illustrated by Helen Bate

Meet Purple Class – there is Jamal
who often forgets his reading book, Ivette who is
the best in the class at everything, Yasmin
who is sick on every school trip, Jodie who owns
a crazy snake called Slinkypants, Leon who
is great at rope-swinging, Shea who knows all about
blood-sucking slugs and Zina who makes a rather
disturbing discovery in the teacher's chair...
Has Mr Wellington died? Purple Class is sure
he must have done when they find a skeleton
sitting in his chair. Is this Mr Wellington's skelington?
What will they say to the school inspector?
Featuring a calamitous cast of classmates,
the adventures of Purple Class will make you
laugh out loud in delight.

ISBN 10: 1-84507-377-0
ISBN 13: 978-1-84507-377-0

Dear Whiskers

Ann Whitehead Nagda

Illustrated by Stephanie Roth

Everyone in Jenny's class has to write
a letter to someone in another class. Only you have
to pretend to be a mouse! Jenny thinks
the whole thing is really silly… until her penfriend
writes back. There is something mysterious
about Jenny's penfriend. Will Jenny
discover her secret?

ISBN 10: 1-84507-563-3
ISBN 13: 978-1-84507-563-7

The Great Tug of War

Beverley Naidoo
Illustrated by Piet Grobler

Mmutla the hare is a mischievous trickster.
When Tswhene the baboon is vowing to throw you
off a cliff, you need all the tricks you can think of!
When Mmutla tricks Tlou the elephant
and Kubu the hippo into having an epic tug-of-war,
the whole savanna is soon laughing at their foolishness.
However small animals should not make fun
of big animals and King Lion sets out to teach
cheeky little Mmutla a lesson…
These tales are the African origins of America's
beloved stories of Brer Rabbit. Their warm humour
is guaranteed to enchant new readers
of all ages.

ISBN 10: 1-84507-055-0
ISBN 13: 978-1-84507-055-7

Roar, Bull, Roar!

Andrew Fusek Peters and Polly Peters
Illustrated by Anke Weckmann

What is the real story
of the ghostly Roaring Bull?
Who is the batty old lady in the tattered clothes?
Why is the new landlord such
a nasty piece of work?

Czech brother and sister Jan and Marie
arrive in rural England in the middle of the night –
and not everyone is welcoming. As they try
to settle into their new school, they are plunged into
a series of mysteries. Old legends are revived
as Jan and Marie unearth shady secrets in a desperate
bid to save their family from eviction. In their quest,
they find unlikely allies and deadly enemies –
who will stop at nothing to keep
the past buried.

ISBN 10: 1-84507-520-X
ISBN 13: 978-1-84507-520-0

Butter-Finger

Bob Cattell and John Agard
Illustrated by Pam Smy

Riccardo Small may not be
a great cricketer – he's only played twice before
for Calypso Cricket Club – but he's mad
about the game and can tell you the averages of every
West Indies cricketer in history. His other love
is writing calypsos. Today is Riccardo's
chance to make his mark with Calypso CC against
The Saints. The game goes right down
to the wire with captain, Natty and team-mates,
Bashy and Leo striving for victory, but
then comes the moment that
changes everything…

ISBN 10: 1-84507-376-2
ISBN 13: 978-1-84507376-318

Hey Crazy Riddle!

Trish Cooke
Illustrated by Hannah Shaw

Why does Agouti have no tail?
How did Dog lose his bone?
Why can't Wasp make honey?

Find the answer to these
and other intriguing questions in this collection
of vivid and melodic traditional tales from
the Caribbean. Sing along to these stories as you
discover how Dog sneaks into Bull's party,
why Cockerel is so nice to Weather no matter
whether she rains or shines, and if the dish
really ran away with the spoon!

ISBN 10: 1-84507-378-9
ISBN 13: 978-1-84507-378-7